COFFEE WITH

ARISTOTLE

C O F F E E   W I T H

ARISTOTLE

JONATHAN BARNES

FOREWORD BY JULIAN BARNES

DUNCAN BAIRD PUBLISHERS

LONDON

Coffee with Aristotle
Jonathan Barnes

Distributed in the USA and Canada by
Sterling Publishing Co., Inc.
387 Park Avenue South
New York, NY 10016-8810

This edition first published in the UK and USA in 2008 by
Duncan Baird Publishers Ltd
Sixth Floor, Castle House
75-76 Wells Street, London W1T 3QH

Managing Editors: Gill Paul and Peggy Vance
Co-ordinating Editor: James Hodgson
Editor: Kirsty Seymour-Ure
Assistant Editor: Kirty Topiwala
Managing Designer: Clare Thorpe

Library of Congress Cataloging-in-Publication Data Available
ISBN-10: 1-84483-610-X   ISBN-13: 978-1-84483-610-9
10 9 8 7 6 5 4 3 2 1
Printed in China

For information about custom editions, special sales, premium and corporate
purchases, please contact Sterling Special Sales Department at 800-805-5489
or specialsales@sterlingpub.com.

Publisher's note:
The interviews in this book are purely fictional, while having a solid basis in historical
fact. They take place between a fictionalized Aristotle and an imaginary interviewer.

CONTENTS

Foreword by JULIAN BARNES

In the Middle Ages, a common male fear—part of a wider apprehension about the world being turned upside down—was of the Woman Wearing the Breeches. From the 13th century onward there are countless decorative representations of one version of this theme. Aristotle and his companion Herpyllis (or Phyllis) are shown in extreme role reversal: the philosopher crawling on all fours like a beast, while his companion rides him sidesaddle, goading him, beating him, and tugging on his philosophic beard. It is a ribald image, but also admonitory: if the most intelligent male who ever lived could be thus overmastered and brought low by woman and the flesh, then none of us is safe.

Nowadays, someone only has to step out of one field of competence into another—a plutocrat flies a balloon across the Atlantic, a cricketer becomes a psychotherapist—for them to be dubbed a Renaissance Man (the Renaissance Woman is more rarely identified). But as the modern two-talent person was to the original multi-skilled Renaissance Man, so the latter was to Aristotle. Even to read this short account of Aristotle's intellectual activities is to be left breathless and envious: breathless at the range, energy and attack of the man; envious for two reasons. First, because he didn't just discover things, but invented entire new disciplines (logic and zoology) while developing many others; second, because he was working and thinking at a time when it still seemed possible for one human being— admittedly, one of the highest mental calibre—to grasp all that could be grasped about the universe. If anyone could, Aristotle could: hence the shock of him being turned into a four-footed ninny.

The author of this book has edited *The Complete Works of Aristotle*, co-edited the four-volume *Articles on Aristotle*, and in the course of his distinguished career has written articles and books on the philosopher. He is also my brother. So if I were to say that the text you are about to read is cogent, learned, accessible, witty and well-expressed, you might not consider the adjectives unprejudiced. On the other hand, this judgment is not lightly given, and has a longer context. His early magnum opus, the two-volume *The Presocratic Philosophers*, gave me a lot of trouble; and I even got bogged down in his more approachable *Aristotle: A Very Short Introduction*. So my praise for this book has some claim to validity.

I asked my brother if Aristotle ever mentioned nepotism—or fraternalism, as in the present instance. Apparently not; though the great man did say, "Brothers are equal in all things, apart from age." This—to my non-specialist eye—seems alas neither memorable nor particularly true. But it reminds me of a complaint that our mother once addressed to a friend: "I have two sons. One of them writes books I can read but can't understand, and the other writes books I can understand but can't read." She agreed with Aristotle in finding us equal, if only in putdownability. However, I suspect that, had she lived, she would have been relieved to discover that one of us has at long last come up with a text that would have satisfied even her.

Julian Barnes

INTRODUCTION

Coffee with Aristotle? Why not? True, he never drank
a cup in his lifetime—nor tasted turkey, or tomatoes,
or tobacco. He lived and died 23 centuries ago. But
his work and his thought did not die. He is in that way
still among us. Coffee with Aristotle, then.

He was a scientist, a historian, a philosopher. Not
many people invent a new science: Aristotle invented
two—zoology and logic. His zoology is outdated—but
modern zoologists admire him, and Darwin said that
Aristotle was his god. His logic, too, is outmoded—
but for more than two millennia Aristotelian logic
was the starting-point of Western thought.

His philosophy was preserved, and sometimes
refined, by his successors. It had an influence on the
astronomy of Ptolemy and the medicine of Galen.
It was—after much controversy—accepted by the

Christian Church, and it became the foundation of medieval scholasticism. It helped to shape Arabic thought. It was admired by the great men of the Renaissance. If it was eclipsed in the 17th and 18th centuries, it shone out again, so that present-day philosophers treat Aristotle not only as a giant among their predecessors but also as an honorary and honored colleague. And we are all influenced, remotely and unconsciously, by Aristotelian thought: when we use such words as "substance" and "accident," "potential" and "actual," "theory" and "practice," we are speaking Aristotle's language.

This interview took place in the last year of Aristotle's life, after he had retired from Athens to his estate on the island of Euboea. It wasn't easy. Everyone knows, more or less, what makes a sports star tick, what hopes and ambitions mark out the life of a politician or a comedian. But a scientist and a philosopher? Their work is often esoteric and their jargon can be baffling. An interviewer needs to keep things simple; but simplicity slips into superficiality—and it is a short step from the superficial to the incomprehensible.

There's another difficulty in the case of Aristotle: we can still read a couple of thousand pages of what he wrote, and we know a fair amount of what he thought; but for his character and his personality we have virtually no evidence—any understanding we may glean on such matters must rely largely on sympathetic imagination.

Aristotle's answers are sometimes brisk, both in content and in style. But briskness was characteristic of the man. The answers are sometimes simple. But pretty well everything Aristotle says here is expressed, at greater leisure and with more detail and subtlety, in his written works.

ARISTOTLE (384–322BC)
His Life in Short

Aristotle died in 322BC at the age of 62. He was survived by his companion, Herpyllis, and by his two children, Pythias and Nicomachus.

His world was slower, and quieter, and darker than ours. And it was a more painful world; for if doctors had a few skills, they had no anaesthetics.

There were no machines. But there were slaves, as numerous as the free population—public slaves who worked the mines, private slaves who worked the fields and who kept the house. Even the poorest families would own a human being or two, and human beings fulfilled the role of machinery at a very modest cost.

There was pain. But there were sophisticated pleasures—and not only for the rich. There was music, and dancing. There were religious and dramatic festivals. Most towns had their theater, which would seat all the local citizenry; and the comedies were often very funny. Then, of course, there was sport, and every four years, the eternal Olympic Games.

It was a pagan world, and religion was everywhere. No corner or crossroads was without its modest shrine. The grandest buildings in the world were dedicated to gods and goddesses, and the blue skies above them were crowded with demons—bad and good. There was no established Church (though the State appointed some of the priests); and there were no Holy Books (though strong traditions preserved ancient myths). But there were public rituals as well as private prayers; and there were public sacrifices. Sacrifices were a chief source of meat—as the gods, to whom the slaughtered beasts were offered, strangely preferred the bones and the offal, leaving the flesh to the worshippers.

It was a small world. A merchant or a soldier might cross the frontiers of Greece, but most Greeks stayed at home, and few knew any language but their own. An inquisitive man would own a library, and his library would easily contain all the Greek that had ever been published—literature, philosophy, history, science. In a couple of years he could read the lot.

Greece was a cultural phenomenon. But it was scarcely a political phenomenon. When Aristotle was born, in 384 BC, the country was divided up into several hundred independent states, some of them no more than hamlets and the largest no bigger than Rhode Island or Monaco. Each had its own laws, its own constitution, its own rulers. There were temporary alliances—against the Persians, for example—but there were also frequent squabbles and occasional wars.

The political face of the country changed in Aristotle's lifetime, when the Macedonians came down like wolves on the fold, and subdued the Greek-speaking world.

———

Aristotle was born at Stagira in Macedonia. His father, Nicomachus, was a doctor to the royal court. His mother, Phaestis, was rich. Both died while Aristotle was a boy, and his maternal uncle, Proxenus, became his guardian. He never worked for his living.

When he was sixteen he moved to Athens, where he joined the Academy—the intellectual circle that buzzed around Plato. The Academicians were omnivores: they busied themselves with ethics and politics, psychology and metaphysics, rhetoric and logic; they worked at geometry and astronomy.

Aristotle was there for two decades. He learned, and later he wrote. Among his favored subjects at the time were rhetoric and logic.

Then, in 347, Plato died. Aristotle left Athens and went east to the township of Atarneus, on the coast of Asia Minor. The ruler, Hermias, was a friend of the Academy and a patron of learning. A historian records that "he gave Aristotle and his friends the town of Assos to live in, where they spent their time in philosophy, meeting together in a courtyard; and he provided them with all they needed." Aristotle was also indebted to Hermias for more personal reasons, for his wife Pythias was Hermias's niece.

After a couple of years at Assos, and another two at Mytilene, on the nearby island of Lesbos, he returned to Macedonia. King Philip had invited him—together with his nephew Callisthenes and his friend Theophrastus—to his court at Mieza to look after the education of the royal son. The prince was twelve or thirteen, and he was called Alexander.

In Asia Minor, one of Aristotle's chief occupations had been zoology—and more particularly, marine biology. In Macedonia, we do not know how he spent his time, his tutoring duties apart; but he was there for seven or eight years.

Alexander inherited his father's crown and set out to conquer the world. Aristotle returned to Athens. In 335 the Academy was under new management, and thriving; but Aristotle established a circle of his own. The members would meet in a public gymnasium known as the Lyceum, where, according to an ancient story, Aristotle would lecture in the mornings to all-comers and talk in the afternoons to his colleagues and friends. He walked as he talked: the Greek for "walk" is *peripatein*—and that (so another ancient story goes) is why his followers were called the Peripatetics. It was doubtless then and there that his major philosophical ideas—on ethics and politics, on cosmology and physics and metaphysics—were fully worked out.

There was grief, too, for Pythias died young. She had given birth to a daughter, who took her mother's name and who later married Nicanor, a cousin of Aristotle. A widower, Aristotle found a companion in Herpyllis, who lived with him until his death. Herpyllis (the Greek name means "grasshopper") is said to have been a servant-girl. She gave birth to a boy, who was named Nicomachus after his paternal grandfather. Nicomachus was killed in battle before he was twenty.

In 323 Alexander died, far away in the East; the Athenians, who had not loved their Macedonian masters, found that it was safe to show their resentment; and Aristotle, whose Macedonian

connections were not a secret, prudently retired
to the island of Euboea, where his family owned an
estate. He was dead within a year. His school, which
he entrusted to Theophrastus, survived at Athens
for some two and a half centuries. His work, which
he entrusted to the world, has survived for more
than two millennia. It was preserved, continued, and
modified by later Greek thinkers—both by men who
proudly called themselves Aristotelians and also by
philosophers and scientists from other traditions
who found it necessary or desirable to adopt a
selection of Aristotelian theories. His writings were
translated into Syriac and Arabic and Armenian—
and Latin. In the Middle Ages his work survived in
Greek and in Arabic in the East and in Latin in the
West; and Aristotle was sometimes condemned but
usually applauded by the Christian Church. If the
Renaissance adored Plato, it esteemed Aristotle; and

that esteem, resisting the attacks of various modern swashbucklers who professed to find Aristotelianism outmoded, has lasted into the 21st century.

———

Aristotle's intellectual interests were unlimited. A list of his writings that probably derives from the catalogue of the celebrated library of Alexandria begins like this:

He wrote a vast number of books, which I have thought it fitting to catalogue here because he was so outstanding in all fields of inquiry: Justice; Poets; Philosophy; Statesmen; Rhetoric (*or* Gryllus) …

The list continues with items on ethics and politics and logic and science and metaphysics and rhetoric and poetics and physics and history and biology and astronomy and optics … It ends thus:

Poems, beginning: "*Holy one, most honored of the gods, far-shooting ...*"; *Elegies*, beginning: "*Daughter of a mother of fair children ...*"

The catalogue is not in any lucid order; it contains some duplicates; and it omits some of Aristotle's most famous works—the *Metaphysics* isn't there. But its size is impressive (the *Collected Works* of Aristotle would have filled some five or six thousand modern pages); and its range is staggering.

Most of the books are lost. The surviving items, which fill fewer than two thousand pages, were organized into a corpus some centuries after Aristotle's death. Unlike Plato's dialogues, they are not polished literary productions—they are supposed to be drafts for the lectures he gave. They are generally terse, abrupt, allusive. They are often obscure and difficult. They do not coruscate. But they have a

strength of thought and a rough vigor of expression
that sets them above most philosophical writings.

———

What of the man himself? What was he like? Come
to that, what did he look like? The evidence is
contradictory: portrait busts show a long face, a deep
forehead, a luxuriant beard, while, according to an
ancient biographer, "he had skinny legs and small
eyes; he wore fashionable clothes, and rings on his
fingers; and he had no beard." The truth escapes
us—and no doubt it doesn't much matter. What
goes for his looks goes also for his character and his
inner life: the various anecdotes handed down from
antiquity are of dubious value, and his own writings
are, for the most part, rigorously impersonal.

But there are a few intimate items: a couple
of poems, a couple of letters, and his last will and
testament. The will begins formally:

All things shall be well; but should anything happen,
Aristotle has made the following provisions: Antipater is
my chief executor in all matters and in perpetuity ...

Antipater, who was the Macedonian governor of
Athens, is given several pages of detailed instructions
in which Aristotle makes provision for his children
and for Herpyllis, settles the future of his slaves
(some of whom are to be freed), and refers to the
commissioning of statues to various members of his
family. These are the last clauses of the will:

Wherever they make my grave they are to take and
deposit the bones of Pythias, as she instructed. And
Nicanor, if he is preserved (which I have prayed for on
his behalf), is to set up at Stagira stone statues, six feet
in height, to Zeus the Savior and Athena the Savior.

NOW LET'S START
TALKING ...

Over the following pages, Aristotle engages in an imaginary conversation covering fifteen themes, responding freely to searching questions.

The questions are in green italic type;
Aristotle's answers are in black type.

THE PUBLIC MAN

Aristotle was brought up at the court of
Macedonia. When he worked in the Greek
East he was the guest of a local ruler, Hermias.
He returned to Macedonia at the command
of the king—in order to tutor Alexander the
Great. In his will he appointed the Macedonian
governor of Athens as chief executor. He moved
among kings and princes; he was close to
political power; and some alleged that all this
went to his head.

Aristotle, you are—so people say—the most eminent
scientist and philosopher of the age, but may we begin
with your public life? For you have also been a public
figure.

A public figure? I don't think so. Of course, I've
known rulers and statesmen—and I've liked some of
them. There's Antipater—he's a close friend. But not
because he's governor of Athens. There was Hermias.
I loved him—but not because he was a prince. He took
an interest in philosophy. He invited me to Atarneus
(that's where he ruled). He was a good man, and
intelligent. Soon after I left, the Persians marched in,
took the place over, and tortured him to death …

Yes, and I remember Themison. He called himself
king of Salamis—a tinpot town in Cyprus. I dedicated
my first book to him. It was an invitation to philosophy,
an invitation he never accepted. Of course, there was

also a real king: Philip of Macedon. My father looked
after his health. I confess that I buttered him up a
bit. I put him into one of my books. It's a dialogue
about death. One of the speakers is anonymous, but
I address him as "most powerful and most blessed of
kings," and Philip knew who I meant.

*And it was through Philip that you made your most
celebrated royal acquaintance.*

Yes, my royal acquaintance ... Alexander. Alexander
the great (as they call him), Alexander the divine
(as he called himself), Alexander the impossible
(as I call him). I tutored him for five years or more.
I was supposed to teach him all I knew—biology
and physics, cosmology and zoology, history and
geography and literature and philosophy. The lot.
Well, I taught him everything—and he learned

nothing. True, some people say that I nurtured his imperial ambitions, and others pretend that I got him interested in nature—they tell a pretty story. They say that when Alexander marched through Persia and Assyria into Afghanistan, he took time off from killing the natives and seducing their women to hunt down exotic beasts, and that he had them sent to me, dead or alive, for an autopsy or a vivisection. Utterly ridiculous. Alexander's interest in animals extended no further than riding or slaughtering them. And did I "nurture his imperial ambitions"? I gave him one piece of advice: Treat Greeks like free men, I said, and treat foreigners like slaves. Well, he treated everyone like slaves. So you might say that I had half an influence over him on that point.

My father was the best of doctors—but he couldn't straighten Philip's twisted leg. I'm the best of teachers—but I couldn't straighten Alexander's twisted

mind. Plato says somewhere that philosophers treat
the troubles of the soul as doctors treat the sicknesses
of the body. Perhaps he's right. One thing's for sure—
philosophers and doctors are equally ineffective.

I wonder if you aren't being too modest …

My dear young man, modesty is one of the few vices
of which I have never been accused.

*Nonetheless, however little you influenced Alexander,
you've been closely associated for most of your life with
the rulers of Macedonia. Isn't that why the Athenians
recently expelled you?*

I left Athens and came here to Euboea by my own
choice. The Athenians didn't officially expel me—
they merely obliged me to leave. Their democratic

grandparents had killed Socrates, and I didn't want
Athens to commit a second crime against philosophy.
They say I'm "pro-Macedonian," and they mean
that I favor the political schemes of the Macedonian
monarchy. But that accusation is perfectly outrageous.
I've hobnobbed with the royals, but I've never
kowtowed. And my political ideals, such as they are,
are quite the opposite of theirs.

You look skeptical—well, you're not the only
one. But read my *Politics*—the proof's there in black
and white. I discuss different sorts of political
constitution, monarchy among them; and I argue
that, on a certain condition, an absolute monarchy
is the best possible form of government. *On a certain
condition*: on condition that the absolute monarch
is a man of perfect virtue. Now since no such man
can ever be found, absolute monarchy is, in point
of hard political fact, a thoroughly vicious form

of government. Philip was absolute monarch in Macedonia: if he'd read my *Politics*, would he have said "Ah, there's a good friend of my government"? As for Alexander, look at the *Politics* again. I claim—for reasons I won't bother you with—that the very notion of a political empire is an absurdity. Alexander's empire covered the whole of Greece and vast tracts of Asia. I've never spoken in support of it—I've denounced it. If that's being pro-Macedonian, what do you have to do to be anti?

My views on monarchy and empire are obvious enough, and I don't claim any particular credit for setting them out. I don't claim any particular courage either—in case you suspect me of virtues as well as vices that I don't possess. Neither Philip nor Alexander were great readers, and in any case if they'd read my *Politics* they wouldn't have cared a jot. Oh, Philip might have guffawed, and Alexander might have stamped his elegant little foot. But cared? Why should they have cared? Words, words, words—they mean nothing in the courts of the mighty.

But you were not just a man of words. You once said that "man is by nature a political animal." Didn't you follow your human nature and take an active part in political life?

The aphorism's mine—though people tend to forget a better one: "Man is more given to copulation than to politics." (Never take aphorisms literally—not even that one.) But no, I've never engaged in political activities.

In Macedonia, I couldn't have—I wasn't one of the ruling élite, and that was that. And during the 30-odd years I lived and worked in Athens I remained a foreigner—I was a "resident alien," or

a *metic*, in their unlovely jargon. I couldn't stand for
political office, I couldn't vote in political elections,
I had no right to be a juryman. I couldn't even buy a
house or a piece of land. I'm not complaining: I chose
to live in Athens, and I don't regret it. In any event,
even if the Athenians had offered me citizenship,
I wouldn't have meddled in politics—I had far, far
better things to occupy my time. You've read my
lectures on *Ethics*?

Well, I've tried …

You've read them "up to a point," eh? Can't say I
blame you. They're pretty arid stuff—like eating
hay, someone once said. Well anyway, those lectures
were delivered to a group of rich young men, a few
of them reasonably honest, some of them quite
clever, and most of them intent on a political career.

I explained to them that politics is a perfectly respectable line for a virtuous man to follow, but that it's essentially a second-best line. It requires you to exercise one part of your mind, and to display one sort of virtue. But it doesn't engage the other and higher part of the mind—it has nothing to do with theoretical knowledge, with knowledge pursued for its own sake. I put politicians a little way above businessmen. But they're not on the same level as scientists and philosophers.

Here's another of my aphorisms: "All men naturally reach out for knowledge." That's the part of our nature that brings us near to the gods.

PLATO, AND RHETORIC

Aristotle was sixteen when he left his parents'
home in Stagira and went south to Athens—
and to Plato's Academy. The Academy was the
intellectual center of Greece: although Plato
devoted himself to philosophy, his circle
included the leading scientists of the day. The
place was famous. (It was lampooned on the
comic stage.) Aristotle stayed there for twenty
years.

Plato must have been a dominating figure. He must have had an enormous influence on you?

He was a giant. But he wasn't a professor: he inspired us and he cajoled us, but he didn't lecture us. What he did was talk—he talked to everyone about everything. We listened … and we talked back. It was marvelous. And it wasn't just Plato, or just philosophy. The cleverest men in the world came to the Academy. I remember Eudoxus, a brilliant astronomer who thought nothing was more perfect than a sphere. A bit of a crackpot? Maybe—but it was from him that I learned all I know about the stars. Oh, and there were mathematicians too, and cosmologists, and even botanists. Despite what he sometimes said about the "so-called sciences," Plato liked nothing better than the company of scientists—and he liked setting problems for them.

But Plato was the central figure, and—for you at least—philosophy was the central subject?

Yes—and that's why I went to Athens. Plato was famous—if you went to the theater to see a comedy, you were likely to hear a joke or two about his ideas. Of course, when I first met him I was overwhelmed. He really cared about *thinking*. I don't mean he gazed at his navel and emptied his mind—he never went in for that sort of nonsense. No: he filled his mind, he gazed about him, his thought was always solid and active. We all venerated him, and we imitated him, and we loved him.

I loved him. "A man whom it is not right for the wicked even to praise"—that's how I described him in one of my poems. Yes, I loved him. But, you know, he wasn't really my type—intellectually speaking, I mean. Let me tell you a story. Once, years ago, he decided (God knows why) to give a public lecture. The day came and the crowds flocked in, two or three thousand of them. He'd announced a lecture on the Good. He started off by talking about arithmetic. After an hour or so the public got a bit restive. He then moved on to geometry. People began to leave in ones and twos. He turned to astronomy ... When he finally got round to the subject he'd announced, he said: "The Good is One." And that was it. He looked up from his notes: there were only four of us left in the theater. He smiled.

I'm different. My feet are on the ground; his head was always in the clouds. I'm a realist; he was, in every sense of the word, an idealist. And as for that lecture—which, I may say, was never repeated—well, as I later said, "Plato is dear to me, but truth is dearer." Of course, he knew what I was like, and he probably thought I was a pompous little donkey. But

he didn't say so—he called me "the Foal." "Why?"
I asked. "Because when a healthy foal is born, the
first thing it does is kick its mother in the belly."

Still, the foal stayed with the mare for twenty
years.

*You mean that it was a love–hate relationship? And
his influence on you wasn't so very important after all?*

No, no. It was a love–love relationship, and he had an
enormous influence on every aspect of my thinking.
Though I saw quickly enough that many of his ideas
were mistaken and some of them simply mad, he
taught me everything about philosophy. Some people
think that a teacher transplants his own thoughts
into his pupil's mind. Well, only bad teachers are
like that. Good teachers aren't gardeners, they're
midwives: they don't transplant their own thoughts,

they help bring to birth the thoughts their pupils have conceived.

Isn't that an idea of Plato's?

Touché—that's one idea he *did* transplant into my mind. But, imagery apart, the point is this: there are more ways of learning from a teacher than taking over his opinions—and one of those ways involves reflecting on his opinions and then rejecting them.

I see. Still, presumably you didn't start out by rejecting everything Plato said? He must have had some more positive effect on you. For example, didn't he direct you along some promising paths of research?

Indeed he did, and the first path he directed me along will surprise you. He told me to think about rhetoric, and his question was this: Is there a *science* of rhetoric? It sounds pretty tedious, doesn't it? Just the sort of question to palm off on someone else. But in fact it had exercised him—he'd quarreled over it with Isocrates, who was the leading rhetorician of the day. No one doubts the importance of being able to speak well, of being able to persuade an audience, to make friends and influence people—in political assemblies, in courts of law, in business meetings, or anywhere else where there are decisions to be made. Well, some men are naturally good at speaking. But others aren't, and one or two clever people realized that there was money to be made: why not *teach* people to speak (for a fee)? And to make it sound impressive, why not teach them the Science of Rhetoric?

Plato didn't much care for all that—apart from anything else, he thought it was unspeakably vulgar to take money for teaching. But he did think that the claim that there is a science of speaking well deserved to be taken seriously. If it turned out to be true, it would have—or so he thought—large consequences for education. In any case, my first job as an apprentice Academician was to take the claim seriously.

And what conclusion did you come to?

I came to a conclusion I almost invariably come to when I'm faced with a philosophical question: the answer is "yes and no." Boring, I know—but if answers are so often like that, that's because the questions are so often badly put. Plato's question about rhetoric presupposes that the capacity to speak well is some single unitary thing, which must either be or fail to be scientific. But that's not so:

in order to speak well, you need to have mastered three quite different things. First, you've got to have style (you've got to know how to choose your words, how to string them together, and so on); then, there's psychology (if you want to persuade the jury to acquit your client, you need to work on their emotions, to make them hate or despise the accuser and feel pity for your own man); finally, you must know how to put an argument together. The first two of those things aren't scientific—the third is. So one part of rhetoric is a science, the science of logic—and that's why the answer to Plato's question is "yes and no."

LOGIC

One of the sciences that Aristotle invented was
logic. He claims, explicitly, to have worked it
up from scratch; and he is right. His logic—his
"syllogistic," as it is usually called—was, quite
apart from anything else, an extraordinary
technical accomplishment: until the middle
of the 19th century it was almost universally
regarded as a complete and perfect science;
and although it is now recognized as only a part
of logic, it is an almost perfect part.

Your work on rhetoric, then, was what led you to logic?
As you know, logic's a daunting subject to most people.
I wonder if you could give a short and simple account of
what exactly it was you invented?

Of course I couldn't. I didn't discover logic one sunny morning in the gardens of the Academy. It took me years of hard thinking, and it would take me hours to explain it. I don't mean that it's fiendishly difficult—it's nothing like as hard as geometry, say. It's not esoteric either—after all, it's the science of reasoning, and we humans are essentially reasoning animals. But it does have a technical side to it, and mastering that demands concentration. Still, I'll do what I can.

It's true, as you've said, that my work on rhetoric led me to logic. But there were two other paths that took me in the same direction. First, there was a game we all played in the Academy. Plato had the idea that we'd become better thinkers if we practiced mental gymnastics. He'd pair us off. One of us had to defend some thesis, the other had to refute him. And—this is the crucial thing—he had to do so not by eloquent speechifying but by posing a sequence of short questions. Thesis: "The universe had a beginning." Question: "Will the universe come to an end?" Answer: "No." Question: "Doesn't everything that has a beginning have an ending?" Answer: "Yes." Q.E.D.

It was a game (we called it dialectic). But it was a serious game—hard study is the sister of play, as Plato put it.

It sounds rather a short kind of game.

Well, it was never as easy as my example may have suggested—some of our sessions went on for hours. But however that may be, I got interested in the theory behind the game. The basic idea was this. The answers supplied the questioner with a number of propositions—a number of premises—from which he might infer certain conclusions; and the conclusions had to follow from the premises. They had to follow *by necessity*: it must be not just odd or eccentric to accept the premises and reject the conclusion—it must be impossible, contradictory, to do so.

Now I thought it ought to be possible to draw up a set of general rules about what conclusions followed—with that sort of adamantine necessity—from what premises. It *was* possible. And that's what logic is—a systematic set of rules of that sort.

You said there was a third path that led you to logic?

Yes. Our scientists—especially the mathematicians among them—were always producing arguments. They weren't playing games (like us young dialecticians), and they weren't in the business of persuading juries or politicians or business partners (like rhetorical reasoners). What they wanted to do was to *prove* things. A geometer, say, would take his stand on a small number of pretty obvious truths (for example, "If two things are equal to the same thing then they are also equal to one another"), and on the basis of them he'd try to establish certain other propositions (such as Pythagoras's theorem). That's the scientific approach: you have certain starting-points (the mathematicians like to call them axioms); and you move on from them to other truths (to theorems, as you might say).

So a question arises: how are you to get from the axioms to the theorems? Is there any method, or theory, or science, that will tell you what you can and what you can't infer from your starting-points?

It was the same question as the one that dialectic had suggested to me. And, of course, it got the same answer.

This scientific path to logic was so much more important than the other two that I came to think of logic as an instrument of the sciences.

An instrument—so that's why your friends call it Aristotle's Organon, *or tool. But are you saying that logic is essentially about* scientific reasoning?

No. Logic is used by the sciences, but it's not confined to scientific reasoning—not by a long way. In fact, it's not confined to any particular sort of subject-matter—that's what dialectic taught me, since there you might have to attack any old thesis. Logic's at home in the scientist's study, and in the mental gymnasium, and in the courtroom—and also, of course, in the sweet solitude of silent thought. It's a universal science.

I don't quite see why you call logic a science—if it's a tool of the sciences, how can it be a science itself?

Ah, that's the wonder of it. After I'd arrived at my code of logical rules, I managed to prove something about it: once you grant that a couple of very simple sorts of argument are valid, then from them you can prove that any number of other sorts are valid. The first couple are the axioms of logic, the rest are the theorems. That's how the tool of the sciences is itself a science—the science of syllogisms.

These are my two axioms:

All Cs are B, all Bs are A: so all Cs are A.
All Cs are B, no Bs are A: so no Cs are A.

Don't be put off by the As and Bs—here's a concrete example of the first one: "Vines are broad-leaved plants. Broad-leaved plants are deciduous. Therefore vines are deciduous."

What do you think of that?

I'm afraid those axioms seem pretty obvious to me.

Of course they do—they're meant to be obvious. Now what about this case: Some Ds are C, all Cs are B, no Bs are A: so some Ds aren't A.

That's not so obvious.

No—but I can *prove* that it's valid just on the basis of my two axioms. And I can do the same thing for any number of other syllogisms—in fact, there's literally no end to the number of them.

I think that's beautiful. Some people have accused me of turning reasoning into a mathematical or a mechanical business. But they haven't understood me at all. Reasoning's like a journey: each move you make is short and obvious; but a sequence of short moves may take you a long way, and a sequence of obvious moves may take you to an unexpected destination. When you get to your destination my rules will tell you whether or not each of your little moves was legitimate; and when you start out you can be sure that you've got all the rules you need to get where you're going. But what my logic can't do is tell you *which* rules you'll need at any given step. No logic can tell you that—you need insight and imagination, and sometimes a touch of genius. That's why good logicians often go haywire when they're arguing about politics or sport or sex.

ZOOLOGY

When Plato died, Aristotle was not chosen to succeed him as head of the Academy. He left Athens and spent the next several years in the eastern Aegean. There, in marine surroundings, he observed the habits of dozens of sea creatures. The observations are recorded in the *History of Animals* and the *Parts of Animals*. (The *History* is not a history, and a better translation of its Greek title is *Zoological Inquiries*.) That work laid the foundations—or parts of the foundations—for the second of the two sciences that Aristotle invented.

On Plato's death, you scuttled off to a remote part of eastern Greece?

When Plato died, it was his nephew who inherited the shop. You think perhaps that I was piqued? Well, I could hardly have posed as Plato's successor, given what I thought of most of his opinions …
In any event, I didn't scuttle: I was invited—by Hermias, who had close contacts with the Academy, who was keen on what I'd been doing, and who offered me splendid working conditions. Still, I doubt if he anticipated what work I'd get up to—nor indeed did I.

You turned from philosophy to science?

I'd always been a scientist—we were all scientists in the Academy. People sometimes talk as if science and philosophy are two quite different activities. That's not how Plato saw it, and it's not how I see it: philosophy is just one science—or one group of sciences—among others. But though I'd always been a scientist, there were some sciences where I knew I'd never make any contribution. In my youth the big sciences were geometry, astronomy, and medicine. I mugged them up; but I had nothing of my own to say about them. On the other hand, there were some sciences—some potential sciences, you might say—where I thought I might make a splash. Logic, of course, was one. Another was zoology—and that's what I turned to when I went to Atarneus.

Weren't there enough animals to look at in Athens?

I went to Atarneus for the fish. It was a fisherman's paradise—and even better was Mytilene, where there was a vast salt-water lagoon. I was keen on animals in general: I wanted to catalogue them, describe them, sort them out into groups, and so on. But what really interested me was how they worked—and from that point of view sea animals have certain advantages. First, they don't run off when you watch them in their natural habitat: you can see how they move, how they eat, how they copulate … Then again, they're easy to anatomize. Cut open a dog (I've done it often enough) and everything is blood and guts; cut open a dogfish (ditto) and the innards are clean and clear. Thirdly, some of these sea creatures are virtually transparent. I love prawns—you can actually see their internal parts in full function. Of course, they're tiny, and they dart about all the time. But if you've got good eyes—and I had excellent eyes—you can discover a vast amount about animal functions just sitting in the Aegean sun and staring into the water.

What about plants—did you look at them, too?

No, I never did much work on plants (my dear friend Theophrastus is the botanist). But I did learn one thing about them during my lagoon-gazing. There are essential differences between animals on the one hand and plants on the other, but it soon becomes quite plain to a lagoon-gazer that in nature there is always continuity. Look at sea anemones: are they animals or are they plants? The answer's yes: they share some features with fish and some with seaweed. That's typical—nature doesn't like gaps.

Isn't there a clear gap between human animals and other species?

What's a man? A featherless biped. That's what Plato said—and then someone showed him a plucked chicken. But he was fundamentally right: men are animals. They're different from dogs, just as dogs are different from horses. They're privileged animals, superior animals, noble pieces of work, and so on. But they're animals, and in the eye of the zoologist they're just one species among thousands.

So you looked at your animals, you cut them open, you wrote them up—you collected an extraordinary number of facts.

Yes—and in science, facts are the foundation of everything. But they aren't enough. Let me explain … but it's getting hot: shall we go and sit over there in the shade by the pond?

SCIENCE AND CAUSES

Scientists, Aristotle said, always look for general
truths—but such truths don't necessarily
hold always and universally. The universe, he
believed, consists of a set of nested spheres
with Earth at the center. The outermost sphere,
or the edge of the universe, is the sphere of
the fixed stars. The innermost sphere is the
sphere of the Moon. In the upper reaches of
the universe everything happens according to
exceptionless laws; but the sublunary part—the
part beneath the Moon—admits exceptions to all
its generalities. Scientists also want to explain
the generalities they discover: they hunt down
the causes of things. And according to one of
Aristotle's more celebrated theories, there are
four different sorts of causes to hunt.

*You were saying that zoologists want more than facts.
I suppose they want universal laws?*

Not quite—they want both less and more than that.
Let's start with the less. A good zoologist looks for
general regularities, not universal laws: his truths
hold, as I put it, "for the most part."

But why?

Well, outside the abstract realm of mathematics and
logic and the divine realm of astronomy, there simply
aren't any universal laws to be had. What happens
beneath the Moon happens regularly—but there are
always exceptions. Sheep have four legs—they're
natural quadrupeds. But do *all* sheep have four legs?
No: some are born defective—and we've all seen five-
legged sheep at country fairs. It's the same in botany.

Olive trees grow vertically—that's their nature. But at the coast you'll see specimens that have been bent and bowed by the winds. The nature of things is regular but it isn't unvarying—differences in climate and environment see to that. Those scientists who look for universality everywhere have failed to see the most characteristic feature of this sublunary world of ours.

So scientists want less than universal laws—but you said that they also want more. I think I can guess why.

You can?

I think they also want explanations or causes. Haven't you said that no one really knows a thing until he's grasped its causes?

That's what I've said. Of course, in fact we know

lots of things without grasping their causes. I know that Alexander conquered half the world—but I can't for the life of me see what caused him to do so. Nonetheless, scientific knowledge—the sort of knowledge that we scientists are searching for—does require a grasp of causes. You must first establish the facts—otherwise you have nothing to explain. But scientists don't simply want to know what happens. (Come to that, they aren't particularly interested in predicting the future or in controlling the phenomena—they leave that sort of thing to prophets and politicians.) What they want to do—what *we* want to do—is to understand things, and that means we want to explain things.

Isn't that rather presumptuous? After all, some philosophers have been rather skeptical about human pretensions to scientific knowledge.

"Perhaps we know nothing at all." "All knowledge is relative." "Science is a social construct." Yes, I know that philosophers have come up with that sort of thing. It's nonsense. Ask your skeptical philosopher why, if he knows nothing, he turns left rather than right when he wants to go to the Academy. Make off with a relativist's wife and tell him that, from your viewpoint, she's not his wife at all … Enough—that sort of stuff makes my blood boil, and it's far too ridiculous to be worth discussing.

Let's return to the cooler ground of causation. You say that scientific knowledge demands a grasp of causes— and you've elaborated a theory of causation.

"Aristotle's Theory of the Four Causes," you mean? It's not exactly a theory—more a classification of the different ways in which we try to explain things.

People sometimes ask "What's *the* cause of this?" and "What's *the* cause of that?" as though things usually had a single cause. But they rarely do: they usually have several causes, or several different types of cause. That's what my "Theory" takes account of.

Just look at those ducks in the pond. Why are they swimming? Well, they swim (rather than sink) because they're made of light stuffs (of flesh and bones, not of lead). They swim (rather than stay still) because their feet are webbed (chickens don't swim), and because they're pushing with their legs (the webs don't work spontaneously). They're swimming toward us (rather than to the other side of the pond) in order to get the bread I've just thrown into the water.

There are your four causes: there's the "matter" (what the ducks are made of), the "form" (their shape), the moving or "efficient" cause (the pushings and pullings), and lastly the goal or "final" cause (what it's all in aid of). I don't mean that everything about a duck has causes of all four sorts—there's no final cause for, say, the color of their plumage. But a zoologist who knows his birds must discover all the pertinent causes of their conditions and activities.

You use the word telos *for the final cause, so that we sometimes speak of teleological causation—and that's something that puzzles me. You said the ducks are swimming in order to get the bread—but do you really think that ducks have goals and intentions?*

Well, I don't think ducks have intentions and plans in the way that we do. But certainly they have goals, and so do most other natural objects. (Time for another aphorism: "Nature does nothing in vain.") Some people profess to believe that the natural world is all mechanical, a matter of push and shove. They're wrong.

Take another example. Why do spiders spin their webs? In order to catch flies. If you haven't grasped that, you haven't understood the first thing about spiders. But you need to be clear about just what it is you've grasped. I don't mean that the gods designed spiders in order to catch flies, and I don't mean that spiders form intentions or say to themselves, "I'm feeling peckish. Let's spin a web and catch a fly." In fact, when I talk about the goals of natural objects, I'm not referring to designs or plans or intentions or anything of that sort. What I mean is simply this: those ducks are swimming here *in order to* get at the bread, spiders spin webs *in order to* catch flies. That's what teleological explanation is—it's encapsulated in the words "in order to." And how could any natural scientist refrain from using those words?

POETRY

The messenger from King Philip of Macedonia arrived with his invitation. Aristotle left his lagoon, to which he never returned. Nor did he ever see Hermias again—a couple of years later the Persians invaded Atarneus and butchered its ruler. Aristotle, who had written an elegy on the death of Plato, wrote again in memory of Hermias. He was not the most gifted of poets; but he theorized about poetry, and his theories were to resonate long after his death.

You were a scientist—and you were also a poet.

A poet? Well, I've put together a few stanzas (who hasn't?). But I'm far too prosaical to be a poet. On the other hand, I *have* written a fair amount *about* poetry, and that, I think, is not bad at all.

There, too, you followed Plato?

There, too, Plato's to blame. He had no poetry in his soul. Of course, he wrote some verses to his boy-friends—who doesn't? But he had no feel for poetry (nor for prose either—but that's another story). Nonetheless, as you say, he did express some pretty strong views on the subject. He managed to persuade himself that poets were dangerous animals—you remember how he proposed to bowdlerize Homer? and how his Ideal State only admitted didactic versifiers and morally uplifting hymn-writers? That was too much for me—in fact, I argued, far from being dangerous, poets are benefactors of mankind.

You mean that they add to the beauty of the world?

That wasn't what I primarily had in mind. Plato, you see, thought that poets were dangerous because they had a powerful effect on our emotions—they make strong men tremble, and stern men weep. Now I couldn't deny that the poets work on our emotions. But I argued that they have a *good* effect on us. I took tragedy as my proof case—after all, the tragedies of Aeschylus and Sophocles and even Euripides are among the most powerful pieces of poetry that have been or ever will be written.

So what happens when you see one of those tragedies? It works on your soul in a variety of ways. Remember the tragedy of Hecuba, Queen of Troy? Her husband was hacked to pieces before her eyes. Troy was sacked by the Greeks. She was taken prisoner, exiled … Well, what's Hecuba to you? And yet, in the theater, you're affected by her sorrows and sufferings—you feel pity for her, you feel fear for yourself and your friends, and so on. They're not full-blooded feelings—and in a way you even get a sort of pleasure from them, something that certainly doesn't accompany real pity or real fear. Still, the feelings are undeniably there, and they're undeniably excited by the poetry.

Yes, I see—but how is that beneficial?

Here's the crucial point: these ersatz emotions have an effect on your real emotions—they cleanse or purge them, as I like to put it. When you take your seat in the theater, you're probably burdened—we all are—with irregular and excessive emotions: you tend to get angry quickly and over nothing, you become euphoric for no good reason … Well, when you come out of the theater, you find that you're in much better psychological health. A physician—a body-doctor—may prescribe an emetic to purge your body; a psychiatrist—a soul-doctor—might prescribe a tragedy to purge your soul. That's the benefit of poetry.

But surely you can't reduce tragedy to a sort of psychological emetic?

I'm not *reducing* anything: I never said that poetry was nothing more than rhubarb or senna or some other purgative drug. If you care to read my *Poetics*, you'll see that I give full weight to other aspects of tragedy—plot, characterization, verse-form, style, music, spectacle ... After all, the study of poetry is what I call a productive art. Just as you do ethics in order to become good, and not just to know what goodness is, so you do poetics in order to produce poetry, and not just to know what poetry is.

And where—apart from Plato—did you find these ideas?

They're deduced from a thorough knowledge of the history of poetry, and of its development. Tragedy, you know, can be studied as though it were a semi-natural phenomenon: it began in a small way (they only used a couple of actors at first); it grew (three actors, then four—changes in the chorus-line, too); and it reached its mature form about a century ago in such masterpieces as Sophocles' *Oedipus Tyrannus*. A mature tragedy has a plot or story that is unified in time and place. The plot concerns a tragic hero—

a noble character who is undone by some unfortunate mistake, or some flaw of character. The play uses a variety of verse-forms and of literary styles. It has a chorus that sings and dances …

Aren't those ideas of yours limited by your historical knowledge? Mightn't there be other forms of tragedy that you Greeks have never hit upon?

Everyone's ideas are to some degree limited by their knowledge—that's inevitable. But I've got enough imagination to see that there *might* be other forms of tragedy. I can imagine a tragedy in which, say, no one danced. I can even imagine a tragedy that wasn't written in verse. All I say is that anything like that—anything that was seriously different from the *Oedipus Tyrannus*—would be a degenerate specimen of its kind: a toothless lion, an oak with a blasted crown.

DEMOCRACY

Aristotle was not a political actor, but he was a political theorist. He was interested in the origins of the state, in the basis of political authority, in the nature of law and the notion of citizenship. But the subject that seems to have concerned him most was the question of how a state should be organized—the question of political constitution. What types of constitution are actually found in the world? What types might in principle exist? What, of all actual and possible ways of organizing a state, is the best constitution?

*You left your fish and your lagoon for Macedonia and
Alexander. As his tutor, one of the things you taught him
about must have been politics?*

I talked to Alexander about politics—about the
theory of politics, I mean. And naturally enough
I found myself thinking a fair amount about the
subject.

And where did your theorizing lead you? You …

"Theorizing"? The word suggests waffle, and I've
never had any time for waffle. My political theories—
like my poetical theories—are backed up by facts: I've
written monographs on the constitutional histories
of some 150 Greek states. What I do is political
science. And it's quite as solid as my studies of bees
(who are also political animals).

Well, then, where did your science lead you? You've said you're not a monarchist and that you have no time for empires. I suppose you're a democrat?

A back-handed sort of democrat, perhaps. I don't think that democracy is the best form of government. I don't even think it's a good form of government— though I did once propose a rather ingenious argument in favor of it. You'd like to hear it? Good.

The Athenians have a special kind of dinner-party—a bring-your-own, where each guest contributes whatever he does best in the way of food and drink. Well, I thought, if everyone brings his best, that must make for a pretty good dinner. So why not think that something similar goes for politics? A democratic assembly is a sort of bring-your-own debate. Each citizen contributes what he's most expert in. So the debate should be well-informed, and the decision that follows ought to be a pretty good one.

What do you think of that?

Very ingenious.

Well, when I explained the idea to one of my Macedonian friends, he asked me if I'd ever been to a bring-your-own dinner-party. I hadn't—so I went to one (I told you that my theories are all based on solid factual research). Yes, you've guessed: it was dire—most people brought along their second-best wines, a few brought the leftovers from their previous night's dinner ("a delicious *pot au feu*"), and so on …

No, I'm not a democrat: democracy is government by prejudice and stupidity. Still, I think democracy's the least bad of the bad forms of government—and that's the best we can reasonably hope for.

You mean that when you have elections, and political parties, and public debate, and all the rest of it, then that will at least guarantee some basic liberties?

I don't mean that at all. Elections have got nothing to do with democracy. You've got a democracy—at any rate, you've got what we Greeks call a democracy—when it's the whole body of the citizens that decides what's to be done. Once you start electing people to make decisions for you, you've got an oligarchy, not a democracy—it's a small group of citizens, not the whole lot of them, that runs the business.

But isn't what you Greeks call democracy quite impracticable?

Not in the least. True, those democratic debates sometimes go on for ever, and some of the speakers seem to inhabit another world from ours. But it's practicable enough: you can easily get five or ten thousand men into a debating-theater.

Five or ten thousand, perhaps. But what if there are fifty thousand, or fifty million?

Fifty *million* citizens? But that's impossible—so, come to that, is half a million. You can't build a ship half a mile long—it couldn't sail. You can't have a state with more than about ten thousand citizens—it couldn't work. States depend on what I call "political friendship": the citizens must know one another, recognize one another, talk to one another. And that puts a limit on the numbers.

Surely no state can have as few as ten thousand citizens?

My dear man, I sometimes wonder where you come from. Of course states can be as small as that. The whole of Greece—the whole of the civilized world—was like that until ten years ago. The biggest Greek state—Athens, of course—had about twenty thousand citizens. (Far too many, and no doubt the reason for the abject condition of Athenian politics.) Even now, the old states are responsible for a good deal of their government—education, festivals, the theater, that sort of thing—though in foreign affairs they all depend on Macedonia.

That reminds me of a point I should have made earlier. I've been speaking as though a state had to be, quite simply, a democracy or an oligarchy or a monarchy or whatnot. That's wrong. Such words as "democracy" and "monarchy" describe different ways of deciding practical questions. Now, there are lots of different sorts of questions that need to be decided in any state—military questions, diplomatic questions, questions about crime and punishment, about religion and culture, about education, and so on. There's no reason in theory why all those questions should be decided in the same way. Quite the opposite, in fact. For example, it's clear that military decisions should be taken by the generals and not by the whole army, let alone by all the citizens.

So the best sort of constitution might be, as it were, part democratic, part monarchic, and so on?

Exactly. But I want to pick up something you said earlier. You suggested that democracy has the advantage of guaranteeing certain political liberties. Our own democrats say the same thing. It's sheer bloody nonsense. Look around you: democracies allow their citizens far less liberty than monarchies do—especially if the monarch is as idle as most monarchs are. And of course, there's no intrinsic connection between democracy and liberty: democracy, as I've said, is a way of deciding questions—it doesn't say what questions are to be decided. Liberty is a matter of what questions are political and what are private. That's quite another matter.

Not that I've much time for liberty myself. In my ideal state everything's fixed by law—for example, there's a law that requires pregnant women to walk five miles every day. Why? Well, it keeps them healthy, they produce healthy babies, and that's good for the state. They're parts of the state, and the parts are there for the good of the whole.

SLAVERY

Even in the most radical of the old Greek
democracies, power was in the hands of the
few—women had no say in things, nor did
resident aliens, nor children, nor slaves.
Slaves made up half the population, and the
whole economy depended on them. In his
Politics Aristotle notoriously defends slavery,
something that his admirers find hard to
stomach.

You don't care for political liberty—and you've
defended the institution of slavery. But in your will
you emancipate your own slaves. Have you come to
take a more enlightened attitude to the subject?

In my will I free some of my slaves, but that
represents the triumph of affection over reason—
quite the opposite of an enlightened attitude. Reason
and enlightenment tell in favor of slavery. Don't
think I say that because I couldn't imagine a world
in which there were no slaves: of course I could—
and in fact some of my contemporaries take what
you call the "enlightened attitude." That's why I
decided to state the obvious and defend slavery.

The matter's simple enough. We all agree that
some human beings—infants, say, or lunatics, or
alcoholics—shouldn't be left to look after themselves.
That's simply because they're not capable of running

their own lives. So we treat them, quite reasonably, in the sort of way we treat dogs or horses: *we* decide what they're going to do—they don't. It's in their own interest—for their own good—that we take the decisions. Quite generally, if a living being is incapable of directing its own affairs, then it's best for its affairs to be directed by someone else. So in particular, any human beings who permanently lack the capacity to direct their own lives—any human beings who are, as I put it, natural slaves—should have their lives directed by someone else. It's rational, it's just, it's in their own interest, that they be slaves.

Come off it, Aristotle: slavery is cruel and inhuman—how can it possibly be in the interests of the slaves?

Cruelty? Do you think I'm cruel to my dogs? Or to my children? Of course, none of my slaves is a friend—a

free man can't be friends with a slave, any more
than with a dog or a child. But I'm fond of them, just
as I'm fond of my dogs and my children. Slaves are
protected by law against cruel masters—just as dogs
and children are. You say that, laws or no laws, some
slaves are cruelly treated? Yes, they are. The same
goes for children. There are vicious fathers, and
there are vicious slave-owners. But that's no more
an argument against having slavery than it is against
having children.

*But you've said that a slave is "a living tool"—isn't that
a positive invitation to maltreatment?*

Quite the contrary: does a carpenter maltreat his
tools? Not if he's sane. Once you think of your slaves
as your tools you'll be more and not less inclined to
look after them. Your tools are your possessions. So

are your slaves. So too, when they're young, are your children. Of course, children—the children of free men—are automatically emancipated once they reach the age of reason. Tools aren't. Nor are natural slaves.

Well, I don't think children are temporary slaves. Nor—come to that—do I think that lunatics and alcoholics should be treated as slaves, even though they can't look after themselves. But even if you were right in theory, surely there aren't more than a small handful of "natural" slaves in the world?

A small handful? It depends on the size of your hands. If you look around, you'll see quite a number of people who are in fact slaves but oughtn't to be. They're not natural slaves, and they should be emancipated at once. But you'll see more people—far, far more people—who aren't in fact slaves but who are constitutionally incapable of directing their own lives. How many of these natural slaves are there? I don't know. But you're one of them—to judge from your accent, you're not Greek, and all non-Greeks are natural slaves.

You're joking. And it's a joke that won't endear you to posterity.

No, I'm not joking. As for posterity, what's it done to endear itself to me?

THE FEMALE OF THE SPECIES

If Aristotle's views on slaves shock, so too
(in many quarters) do his views on women.
Whereas Plato had suggested that there are no
significant natural differences between men and
women when it comes to running their lives or
running for public office, Aristotle maintained
that women are intellectually inferior to men,
and that even Greek women (though they're
not natural slaves) are unfit by nature to make
practical decisions, whether public or private.

Posterity will judge you wrong about slaves—and also,
I think, about women. Unless I've misunderstood you,
you think that women are, as it were, half-slaves?

You haven't misunderstood me. And please
don't remind me that Plato—for once—held an
"enlightened" view on the matter. That's because
he wasn't a zoologist. I am. I know something
about female animals.

It's all about sex, of course. Ever since I was a
boy, I've been fascinated by sex. Why do animals
come in different sexes? What's the *point* of sex? I
remember putting the question to Herpyllis once …
Still, it's clear that pleasure can't be all there is to
sex (after all, you only need one sex for pleasure—
and animals have two); and it's just as clear that sex
has something to do with reproduction. (I mean,
reproduction is evidently its goal or final cause.)

But there's a difficulty. It seems that you don't need different sexes for reproduction any more than you do for pleasure. After all, my gardening friends assure me that plants are sexless, and they get on all right; and the fishermen around my lagoon told me that the same is true of lots of animals—mussels and oysters, for example.

How could I get around that difficulty? Well, at first I was tempted by the flower-pot theory.

The what?

The flower-pot theory. It goes like this. The female of the species doesn't contribute anything to the offspring: the whole of the offspring derives from the male. The female provides a sort of flower-pot or seed-bed in which the offspring starts to grow.

It's a nice theory. But, as I quickly saw, it won't

wash. It's perfectly plain that offspring inherit from their mother as well as from their father. I had a randy little bitch once—she'd mate with any dog who sniffed her up. The puppies—luckily for them—all took after mama.

That's quite fascinating, but can we come back to your views about women?

You're right. I chatter on—old age, I suppose. Yes, puppies may resemble—generally do resemble—both the male and the female parent. So the flower-pot theory won't work. Actually it doesn't even work for plants. Despite what the gardeners say, plants aren't sexless—it's just that most of them are hermaphroditic.

No—don't stop me—I'm coming back to women … Well, for reproduction you need, generally speaking, a pair of animals, and the two must be interestingly different. (By the way, why are there are only two sexes—why not three, or seven? Life would be more complicated, no doubt. But more exciting, too, don't you think?) Anyway, what, I next wondered, are the principal differences between the two sexes? One thing struck me at once: in most species, the male is better finished than the female—compare the plumage of a peacock and a peahen, compare the tusks of a boar and a sow, compare the large king bee* to the little female workers. If you look a bit more closely, you'll see that females are often like castrated males. Castrate a bull and it doesn't develop like an ordinary male—bullocks low like cows. It's the same with human animals: eunuchs—Hermias was a

---

* Editor's note: the queen bee was universally thought to be the king until the 16th century, when it was discovered (in Spain) that the ruler of the colony was female and produced all the other bees.

eunuch, so I know what I'm talking about—eunuchs have high voices and soft skins, are relatively hairless, and so on. In a word, they're feminine. So, to put the same thing the other way round, women are like eunuchs—they're unfinished men.

Of course, these things are all matters of degree.

You mean that, in a way, there aren't two sexes, but a sort of graded scale, from very masculine to extremely feminine?

I couldn't have put it better myself—it's another case where nature detests discontinuities. But let me take the argument to its conclusion. Females, we observe, are like imperfect or underdeveloped males. Now, one of the last parts of a human animal to mature is its mind—its capacity to think and to reason. Hence, female humans are less capable of reasoning than males. That's one of the chief differences between the sexes—as evident, and as biologically determined, as the difference between their reproductive systems. That's how women are, so to speak, semi-slavish by nature. That's why they can't direct their own lives. That's why they can't take any part in political affairs—nor, of course, in scientific inquiries.

ETHICS

Aristotle maintained that political theory and
ethical theory go hand in hand, and that ethics—
like politics—is a science that aims not only to
uncover the truth but also to change or affect
behavior. Aristotle's ethical thoughts are directed
at young men, rich and well-born, and they
center on two things: human happiness (his word
is *eudaimonia*), and the virtues (the *aretai*) on
which happiness depends.

You tried to teach Alexander some politics. You must also have tried to teach him ethics—to curb his vices and encourage his virtues?

I tried, yes … He was naturally prone to some virtues—no one ever questioned his courage. And some vices held no attraction for him—modesty, say. But in other departments …

Perhaps you had more success as a theoretician than as a counselor? I suppose you taught him your celebrated Doctrine of the Golden Mean?

It's curious how you become famous for things you never dreamed of. There's no such thing as Aristotle's Doctrine of the Golden Mean. True, there *is* something you might call a "doctrine of the mean." But there's nothing golden about it. And—as I thought my *Ethics* had made perfectly clear—it's utterly trivial. The doctrine, since you ask, says that every moral virtue lies at a mid-point between opposed vices. What does that mean? Well, the "mid-point" isn't a geometrically middle point, and it isn't a point of moderation either. The doctrine amounts to this: In order to be virtuous, don't do or feel either too much or too little. It's as though a doctor advised you to take "the appropriate amount" of the medicine—not too much and not too little. True advice—but not very helpful. That's why I call the doctrine trivial.

What you need to know is *how much* medicine is appropriate (for you, here and now), and *what* (for you, here and now) is the right thing to do or feel. For that, there are some rules of thumb—don't drink yourself stupid every evening, be generous to your friends when they need you, don't run away at the first sight of the enemy, and so on. Apart from that, you have to use your moral sensibility—a philosopher can't do anything for you.

Then what's the use of a philosopher in ethics?

Well, let me summarize what I'm up to in my *Ethics*. Bear in mind that it's supposed to be a practical work (we want to become good, not just to learn what goodness is), and that it's addressed to young men of good families (there's nothing in it for women or for workers).

Here I go. "The question before us is this: How are you young men to make a success of your lives? How are you to flourish, to be happy? The answer is neither long nor difficult to comprehend. For you, to be happy, or to flourish, is to be a good human being, a finished example of the species *Homo sapiens*. Now being a good so-and-so is a matter of having, and consistently acting upon, the excellences or virtues that are characteristic of so-and-sos. It follows that, for you, to flourish is to live in accordance with the characteristically human virtues. We know that there are two types of human virtue: there are virtues of character ('moral virtues,' as they're usually called) and there are virtues of intellect. The virtues of character include courage, generosity, justice, friendliness, wittiness … The virtues of intellect include intelligence, knowledge, wisdom, acuity … The intellectual virtues are superior to the virtues of character. That is why a life in accordance with them—a life of scientific and philosophical study—is the best form of human life. But not all of you are capable of such a way of life. Some of you must be content with the second best, living according to the virtues of character—which you will best do if you engage in political life."

There, in a nutshell, is my ethical theory—set down in my best professorial style. (It's so much more fun going to the theater than listening to a philosophy lecture.)

These virtues—I think you call them dispositions or inclinations to act in certain ways?

Virtues are inclinations, yes—and so too, of course, are vices. But they're not just inclinations to act. My "doctrine" of the mean talks about doing *and feeling*: virtues (and vices) are inclinations to feel as well as to act.

You mean that to be virtuous you must eliminate or master your emotions?

No—that's just what I *don't* mean. Take fear. It's the

emotion involved in courage. We sometimes say that brave men are fearless, but taken literally that's false. A soldier who isn't afraid of having a spear stuck through his groin isn't brave—he's insensible, and there's no virtue in that. You shouldn't try to eliminate your fears. There are plenty of things it's utterly rational to be afraid of. You shouldn't try to master your fears either. A brave man isn't someone who trembles like a jelly inside but manages to bottle it up and get on with the job. That's what I call self-control. It's better than nothing. But it's not a virtue. A brave soldier is very often afraid. But he doesn't have to master his fear—he acts *with* his fear, not in spite of it.

Perhaps the point's easier to see in the case of love. You'll agree that it would be insane to suppress all feelings of love. But equally, it's not good if you have, so to speak, to master your love—if you have to force yourself to act in the appropriately loving way when you really don't feel much love, or when you are overwhelmed with passion. A good lover has the right amount of love—for his children, for his friends … And of course the right amount isn't necessarily a moderate amount: who thinks well of a mother who has a moderate love for her children?

I see. So your young men must acquire and practice the virtues in order to become good specimens of Homo sapiens. *But suppose they don't particularly* want *to be good specimens of* Homo sapiens?

Oh, but they *do*. They certainly want to make a success of their lives—who doesn't? And how can you make a success of your life—of your human life—except by being a good specimen of *Homo sapiens*? Don't tell me that people find happiness in gaining money, or in writing a poem, or in winning a crown at the Olympic Games. They do, of course, but those things don't compete with the virtues—either they're necessary conditions for virtue (it's not easy to be generous, for example, if you're poor) or else they're manifestations of virtue (the poem exhibits your intelligence and insight and whatnot).

But what if, in the end, your young men really want not what you call success or happiness but rather a life of uninterrupted pleasure?

In that case, they're no better than cows—and I don't lecture on ethics in a byre.

METAPHYSICS

When in 336BC Alexander succeeded his father
to the Macedonian throne, Aristotle went back
to Athens, where he founded an intellectual
circle of his own. It was during his second
Athenian period that he worked out his views on
what modern philosophers call "metaphysics."
The sense of that word (for which Aristotle
himself had no equivalent) is not immediately
apparent, and in fact different philosophers
have understood different things by it. It will be
best to let Aristotle speak for himself.

The Ethics *is one of your most renowned works. Another is the* Metaphysics. *I know that philosophers rave about it—but I confess that I found it pretty hard going.*

Metaphysics? Never heard the word. Still, I can guess what you're thinking of.

There's a science that I call (unimaginatively enough) "primary philosophy"—I didn't invent it, but I was the first to see that it's a genuine science. It's unlike other sciences insofar as it deals with absolutely everything. Ornithology looks at birds, arithmetic deals with numbers, and so on. But primary philosophy doesn't cut off a part of reality: it looks at reality as a whole—it's the science of everything that exists. I think of it as having two parts. First, it catalogues—it draws up a list, in the most general terms possible, of what sorts of things exist: physical objects, their parts, their qualities, their relations; abstract entities, such as numbers and geometrical shapes and propositions; events, such as speeches and games and battles. The list has a hierarchical organization. It's clear that, say, cats and colors exist all right; but they don't exist in the same way. Colors exist inasmuch as some things—such as cats—are colored, but cats don't exist inasmuch as some other items are catlike. Cats, as I put it, are *substances*, they're fundamental parts of the world.

The second part of primary philosophy is descriptive: it tries to set out—in as systematic and scientific a way as possible—all the truths that hold of absolutely everything on the list. For example, absolutely every existent thing is *one* thing, it's *the same* as itself and different from other things, it's either a *substance* or an *accident*, it may be *actual* or *potential*, it has an *essence* and a *definition*, it's either colored (say) or not colored (and not both at once) …

Wait a minute. Some people might think that half what you've just said is jargon ("substance," "essence," and so on), and that the other half is trifling—I mean, isn't it dazzlingly obvious that everything is one thing?

I plead guilty to jargon—after all, new ideas sometimes need new words. But the other half isn't trifling. You think it's "dazzlingly obvious" that everything is one thing? I don't—if only because it's not obvious what counts as being one thing. Here's a simple example of what I mean. Look at that goat over there: is it one thing? Well, it's one goat. (Come to that, it's one mammal, one animal—in fact, it's any number of one things ... But that's another question.) Yet it's also made up of a body (the flesh you can eat and the bones you can grind up for bone-meal), and of a soul (the bit you can't eat or grind up and which shows itself in the feelings and thoughts and desires that make up a goat's life). So isn't it really *two* things?

There surely *are* two things there—one goat-body and one goat-soul. Plato (I keep coming back to him)—Plato thought that the real goat—the goat beneath the skin—is the goat-soul. The goat-soul just happens to be wearing a body in the way in which a body might wear clothes. But that can't be right: a body and its clothes don't make up one thing—a soul and its body do. The goat, body and soul together, is *one* unified item. But what makes it one? And why isn't a nightdress and a naked body *one* item? That's a question that continues to baffle me.

You've made your point. But can you say a little more about the first part of your primary philosophy?

Some people pooh-pooh it. "What exists?" you ask.

"Easy," they answer: "everything." Of course, they're right—but there's much more to it than that. The cataloguing itself isn't easy, but it's the hierarchical organization that's really perplexing. Here's an example—I cracked my brain over it for decades.

Will the catalogue include numbers? Of course it will. Numbers exist—there are eleven of them between 57 and 69, say, and infinitely many of them *in toto*. No one's going to pretend that, really, there aren't any numbers. The difficulties start when you try to explain *how* they exist. Plato thought they were substances existing separately from ordinary everyday objects. In his view, numbers are a bit like rulers: if you want to measure a plank of wood, you take a ruler, which exists quite separately from the plank, and set it alongside the plank. So too, he thought, if you want to count the ducks on the pond, you take the numbers, which exist quite separately from the ducks, and you match them up with the ducks.

I couldn't believe that. Numbers are like sizes—they're a sort of quantity. Sizes exist all right—things come in different ones. But sizes exist insofar as things have a certain size. And numbers, I think, exist insofar as things have a certain plurality. There's a number seven insofar as there are exactly seven ducks on the pond. Something like that *must* be right. But the matter's far from straightforward. I mean, if numbers are, as I think, properties of things, then what are they properties of? Of the ducks? No: each duck is one duck, not seven. Of the flock? No: it's one flock, not seven. Of the ducks as a group? But what's that if it's not the flock?

There are lots of questions there—I only wish I could answer them.

THE SOUL

The entities that Aristotle's primary philosophy studies come in all sizes and shapes; but the basic items—the substances—are material bodies, animal, vegetable, and mineral. In the heavenly regions these substances are made of a special stuff called aether; in the sublunary world they are composed of the four elements: earth, air, fire, and water. Of these bodies some are inanimate and some are animate—some don't and some do possess a soul.

Among the entities that your primary philosophy
catalogues, there are—unless I've misunderstood
you—immaterial as well as material things?

That's true. After all, there are shadows. They're
not material objects—they don't weigh anything.

And there are also souls?

Of course. After all, everyone agrees that all living
things—plants as well as animals—have souls.

Everyone?

Ah, I see—you're used to thinking in a barbarian
language. Pity. In Greek, one normal word for
"living" derives from the word for "soul," so that to
us it's as obvious that living things have souls as it is

that breathing things have breath. Shame all languages aren't as perspicuous as Greek. Anyway, living things are ensouled, ensouled things possess souls: *ergo* (as we logicians say) living things possess souls. That's trifling—it's like saying that husbands possess wives. What's *not* trifling is the answer to the next question: just what are these souls that living things possess?

It was here that my predecessors went wrong: some of them guessed that a goat's soul was a small fire stoked up somewhere within its body, others thought that it was the blood that warms the cockles of its goaty heart, and so on. Plato was no better: he thought that it was a ghostly, incorporeal substance temporarily installed in the goat's body. It's not simply that those are wrong answers to the question "What's a soul?"—they're the wrong *sort* of answer.

So what's the right sort of answer?

It goes like this. A soul is what makes the difference between a living and a non-living item. Well, what *is* the difference? It consists in the fact that living items can do some things that non-living items can't, that living items have certain abilities or capacities. Call them "vital capacities." At the lowest level—the level of plants—the vital capacities are the powers of nutrition, growth, and reproduction. Olive trees eat and grow and reproduce (and die): opals don't. Then there are the perceptual capacities—or rather, the five different sensitive capacities: sight, hearing, taste, smell, touch. Ostriches see things—olives don't. There's also the power to move. And finally, there's a capacity, or rather a batch of capacities, that's pretty well reserved for human animals—I mean the power of thought, in all its varied forms. An ensouled item is simply an item that has all or some of these vital capacities. And a soul isn't a lump of stuff, nor even a lump of non-stuff—it's a set of capacities.

Then souls are immaterial parts of plants and animals?

They're immaterial—you can't use a capacity as a door-stop. But they're not parts. The goat-body and the goat-soul, as I said before, together constitute a single item—a goat. But soul and body don't make up the goat in the way in which four fingers and a thumb make up a hand. A saw is a serrated bit of metal that has the power to rip through wood: it's a single item constituted by the metal and the power—but I don't think you'd say that the power was a *part* of the saw. Well, souls and bodies are like that.

These vital capacities are fascinating things, and I've spent many years thinking about them. Locomotion, for example. I once proved that all animals must have an even number of legs. But there's much more to locomotion than legs. What happens when the duck swims for the bread? Two things seem pretty clear, don't they? First, the duck must *see*—or somehow perceive—the bread (if it didn't, it wouldn't move toward it). Secondly, it must have some sort of *desire* for the bread (otherwise, once again, it wouldn't move its webbed feet). And, of course, the perception and the desire must collaborate with one another. At bottom, the recipe is this: perception plus desire equals action. It's the same for human action—except that, with human animals (and a few others), thought and imagination may take the place of perception. A man doesn't have to *see* a piece of bread in order to go to the bakery.

You tried to explain the other vital capacities, as well as the capacity for locomotion?

Yes—and I got interested in a few side-issues, too (dreaming, for example, and remembering). I doubt if what I said about thinking will convince many people (to tell the truth, it scarcely convinces me). But I got things more or less right about perceiving. It's evident that perception is a causal interaction between a perceiver and an item perceived. When a bonfire warms your face, there's a causal interaction between the fire, or some part or aspect of it, and your face, or some part or aspect of it. It's the same when a nettle stings your hand. Or when you see a duck: the duck, or some aspect of the duck (its color and shape, say), has an effect on you, or on some part of you (on your eyes, say). And that's what it is for you to see the duck.

Perhaps you think that's another dazzlingly obvious fact? Well, it wasn't obvious to Plato. Things that are obvious once you've seen them are often difficult to see for the first time.

GODS

Aristotle's universe is topped by divinities.
He advanced a complicated argument to prove
that there must be an "Unmoved Mover," or a
divine First Cause, of the world. The highest
object of study, he claims, is the divine. And
when in the *Ethics* he advocates the theoretical
life, that is in part because it is the life of the
gods, so that in living it we do the best we can
to "immortalize" ourselves. Aristotle's gods are
eternally contemplating things; but they don't
do anything—they're not productive (they didn't
make the world), nor are they provident (they
don't look after the inhabitants of the world).

In your will you leave money to pay for statues of Zeus and of Athena. Are you a religious man?

I believe in gods, in divinities—who doesn't? I take part in the festivals—who doesn't? I admire the temples—they are glorious works. And yes, I'm paying for a couple of statues. But do I *believe* in Zeus and Athena and the rest of the pantheon? I don't believe that a rainbow is an appearance of the divine Iris, or that when it thunders, that's Zeus farting. I don't believe that, somewhere up in the sky, there's another country, populated by beings who once made the world and everything in it and who still take an interest in what goes on down here. I don't believe that anyone up there takes notice of our sacrifices or listens to our prayers.

But still, you believe in the gods?

I believe that the heavenly bodies—the Sun and the Moon, the planets and the stars—are divine. They move, eternally and invariably, in perfect circles; and whatever is perfect is divine. That's evident. I also believe—and this is something I've proven—that behind the heavenly bodies, which move, there are immobile items which move them, and which are thinking, perfectly and perpetually, of themselves. They too are divine. Yes, I believe in gods.

But it would be folly—worse, impiety—to imagine that these gods were, so to speak, supermen. They're not even semi-human: they haven't got bodies like ours, and they don't act. In fact, they don't *do* anything. The world is eternal and needed no creating; it's self-running and doesn't need anyone to keep it going. We rightly admire the gods. And for the same reason we're right to imitate them to the best of our abilities. But praise to the holiest in the height? No—let us praise famous men. Praising the gods is as absurd as praising the axioms of geometry. Pray to the gods? Pray to powerful men—what they do makes a difference to you and what you say may just make a difference to what they do. But the gods can neither hear nor answer your prayers.

You have a theology, but no religion?

That's a nice way of putting it.

But there's one aspect of the theology I still don't understand. Your gods don't do anything, and yet you call some of them Unmoved Movers. Isn't moving a sort of doing?

I've not been clear enough. Let me try again. There are three points. One: the universe is a lovely and a complicated thing. But though we tell the time by its revolutions, it's not a vast clock, and you shouldn't look for a maker's name. Two: the gods don't have anything to do with the day-to-day running of the world. Things happen by nature—that's to say, they happen invariably above the Moon and regularly below it, and they happen like that because of their own natures and not because of any outside influence. Three: nevertheless, the gods are movers, and they move things in this world of ours. The heavenly bodies do so visibly—for example, the Sun warms the soil thereby causing the wheat to sprout. As for the Unmoved Movers, they are final causes: they move things in the way in which objects of desire and of love move things. The trees strain upward to the heavens, the sunflower turns each day to follow the course of the Sun. All nature strives after the Unmoved Movers. Most things do so unconsciously—

but we, or at least the best among us, consciously do whatever we can to immortalize ourselves.

That sounds strange.

Should theology sound familiar?

DEATH

The gods are immortal; and men should strive
to "immortalize" themselves—by imitating
the gods to the best of their abilities. But they
can't do so literally: all men are mortal. Plato
disagreed. Death, he said, is a separation of
the soul from the body; and Plato's soul, which
is the real Plato, survives death—and lives on
for ever. Aristotle's views about the nature
of the soul put any sort of survival—let alone
immortality—out of the question.

Like any philosopher, you must have thought about death.

I've thought a bit about death—who hasn't? But I can't say that I find the matter particularly gripping.

Plato was different—again. He had some fairly bizarre opinions on the subject. He thought that when we die our souls disembark from our bodies and march off to a Court of Justice. The judges examine our past lives, find us innocent or (more likely) guilty, and pass sentence. If we're innocent, we live on forever in immaterial bliss, and if we're guilty, we're condemned to another corporeal life (perhaps in a human or perhaps in a bestial form); and at the end of that life, the same thing happens all over again. I doubt if many people have swallowed the whole of Plato's story—but an enormous number seem to have swallowed the general idea. And yet neither Plato nor anyone else can find the slightest reason in support of such fantastical notions.

If you're looking for immortality, the divinities are immortal. So too is the universe—and all the natural species it contains. There always have been dogs and dandelions, and there always will be. In that way, the human race too is immortal. But individual humans—like individual dogs and dandelions— aren't.

Then you don't think that there's any survival after death?

Well, we all live on for a while in the memories of our family and friends (and of our enemies). But that won't last more than 50 or 60 years. A very few of us survive in another sort of way. Homer survives in the *Iliad* and the *Odyssey*, and Alexander, I'm sure, will survive in any number of romances. Perhaps that's not what you mean by survival? Let's not quarrel about words. Survival or not, isn't it something worth having? If I had to choose between living on in my works for a couple of thousand years and coming back to Earth from time to time in the form of an ape or a peacock, I know what I'd opt for.

I'm not so sure … In any case, apart from that sort of quasi-survival, death is the end of everything?

Yes. There's no mystery about it. We see death every day, and we know what it's like. That willow aslant the brook is dead. You've just killed a fly. And to judge by the smell, there's a dead rat or perhaps a dead dog in the neighborhood. When things die, we sometimes say, their souls separate from their bodies. But what does that mean? It means that an animal or a plant dies when it loses its vital capacities, when it can't any more feed, or grow, or reproduce, or move, or perceive, or think, or feel … That stinking dog—I think it's a dog—became a corpse a day or so ago. It ceased to be able to sniff and run after rabbits. It's an ex-dog. Bits of it will last longer than other bits, and its bones will stay around for a very long time. But the *dog*—the dog doesn't last.

Nor of course does the dog's soul. How could it? How could a capacity outlast the thing that has the capacity? "The wine's all gone," a friend said to me once, "but perhaps its capacity to intoxicate is still in the bottle." He was a little tipsy at the time—but it was a good joke. It's just as much a joke to suggest that the dog's capacity to sniff or to chew a bone might outlast its nose or its jaws.

That's what happens to animals—to human animals no less than to the others. It'll shortly happen to me. This bag of bones you've nearly finished cross-examining will very soon be incapable of functioning: no more talk, no more thought, no more perception … Aristotle's history will come to an end.

Isn't that a bleak and terrifying prospect?

I don't *want* to die. I've still got most of my teeth (if other parts of me no longer work as well as they once did). I can still see the colors and the forms of nature (though my eyes aren't up to marine biology any more). I can still hear most of what people say to me (not that that's an unmitigated blessing). And, of course, I can still reason—as brilliantly as ever. So life's a boon, and I don't want to leave. But it's one thing not to *want* to die, quite another to be *afraid* of death. And I can't say that I find being dead a terrifying prospect—it's more like no prospect at all.

Some ways of dying are frightening—a lingering disease, a festering wound, a drawn-out mental and intellectual decline. It's reasonable to be afraid of those things. But being dead? It's only rational to be afraid of something (a snake, say, or a surgical operation) if you think it's likely to hurt you in some way or other—the snake may sink its fangs into your leg, the operation is sure to be excruciatingly painful. But nothing hurts the dead. You can cut that canine corpse open, and it won't yelp with pain. You can curse it, and it won't put its tail between its legs. It feels nothing. It *can't* feel anything. It had no reason to be afraid of being dead. Nor have I. Nor have you.

PROSPECTS

After Aristotle's death his school was taken over by Theophrastus, who worked to fill the gaps Aristotle had left and to perfect the sciences he had promoted. The school was busy for a century or so, and then fell into a somnolence. It awoke toward the end of the 1st century BC, and from then until the end of antiquity—indeed, until the end of the Middle Ages—Aristotelianism, in one form or another, was a living and often the dominant system of thought. Not all of Aristotle was equally prized: his zoology and his politics were relatively little read. But other areas—most notably his logic, his cosmology, his physics, and his metaphysics—became fundamental parts of Arabic and of Western civilization.

You believe that you will not literally survive your death. But you hope for a quasi-survival in your works. Which of them do you think are most likely to last?

Hard to say ... My *Analytics*, surely—for as long as anyone retains any interest in logic. After all, I not only invented the subject, I virtually perfected it, and I can't imagine that anyone will ever find much more to discover in the way of logic. As for the rest, I'm not so sure. No doubt my general picture of the world will be accepted: no one's likely to challenge the view that the universe is finite and spherical, that the Earth lies at its center, that things below the Moon are made of the four elements, that above there is the aether and the Unmoved Mover ... All that's established fact. Still, I don't think many future physicists will read my *Physics*: they'll have their textbooks, and my views will no longer be mine—they'll be commonplaces.

And what of your detailed scientific work?

My zoology? Well, if I perfected logic, I barely
scratched the surface of zoology. I didn't investigate
all known forms of animal life—and no doubt there
are unknown species in the antipodes that are quite
unlike anything here. Not only that: even when I
went deeply into a subject, I was aware that there
were further depths to be plumbed—at the end of
my very detailed description of bees, for example,
I allow that future apiculturalists may come up
with observations that show that my theories need
modification. Then again, there's such a lot I simply
couldn't observe. If only there were instruments
that made our eyes as powerful as the eyes of a lynx
and our noses as sharp as the noses of hunting-dogs
… In any case, I never got remotely near a unified
and systematic science of animal life: compared to

geometry, my zoology is a baby. No—I like to think that people will go on reading my *History of Animals*, but they'll read it as a historical monument, not as a part of living science.

Your philosophical writings?

My *Ethics* won't date. After all, it's based upon a solid knowledge of human nature—and human nature won't change. My *Politics* will be forgotten. It was written for a world consisting of states, and thanks to Alexander there are no states any more—everything is just too big. *On the Soul*? My stuff on primary philosophy? … I don't know. But I'll make one prediction. Those of my philosophical works that *do* survive will survive among the professionals. Plato's dialogues, I'm sure, will be read by pastry-cooks: I'll only be read by philosophers.

Has your life been a success? Has it met the standards you set in your Ethics?

Don't ask whether a life has been successful until it's over—after all, there's still time for the Athenians to condemn me to death ... Not that that would be so very important. But imagine that on my death my books and papers were destroyed, and no one ever took any of my projects any further. In that case, my life—much of it—would turn out to have been in vain ... True, it's a remote possibility, and I haven't lost much sleep over it.

In any case, there are some things no one can take away. There's my logic—I'm sorry to harp on about it. But that's *one* thing of which I'm rightly proud. Then there's my work on chronology—the lists of winners in the theatrical competitions at Athens, the lists of victors in the games at Delphi.

We haven't talked about that.

No—but it's not unimportant, you know. The work
was pretty tedious—long hours in dusty archives.
But the results are worth it: they give historians
a stable chronological framework—and without
that they can't do very much in the way of history,
can they? Yes, that's another thing I'm proud of.
The Delphians were pleased with it, too. They
honored me with one of their fancy inscriptions:
"The Amphictyons"—that's their word for the local
officials—"The Amphictyons declare that Aristotle,
son of Nicomachus, from Stagira …" and so on. A
couple of months ago, when Alexander died, they
changed their tune: they stripped me publicly of
the honors, and they broke up the inscription.

Postscript

In 1898 German archaeologists working at Delphi rediscovered the inscription honoring Aristotle: they found it at the bottom of a well-shaft, smashed to pieces. This is the text:

[THE COUNCILORS OF DELPHI DECREE THUS: SINCE THEY HAVE DRAWN UP A LIST] OF THE VICTORS AT THE PYTHIAN GAMES, LET US PRAISE ARISTOTLE AND CALLISTHENES AND CROWN THEM. AND LET THE STEWARDS SET UP A COPY OF THE LIST [IN THE TEMPLE …]

Text within square brackets comprises words not preserved on the stone fragments, but the general sense of the restoration is certain.

NOTES

References to works by Aristotle cite page, column, and line of a standard edition of the Greek text of Aristotle, which all later texts, translations, and commentaries make use of.

p.17 "he gave Aristotle..."
Philodemus, *History of the Academic Philosophers*, V 7–13.

p.18 according to an ancient story
It is told by Aulus Gellius, *Attic Nights*, XX 5.

pp. 21 and 22 "He wrote a vast number..." / **"Poems, beginning ... fair children ..."** The list is transmitted by Diogenes Laertius, *Lives of the Philosophers*, V 21–27.

p.23 "he had skinny legs ..."
See Diogenes Laertius, *Lives of the Philosophers*, V 1.

p.24 "All things shall be well ..." / **"Wherever they make my grave ..."** The will is preserved by Diogenes Laertius, *Lives of the Philosophers*, V 11–16.

p.33 "man is by nature a political animal" *Politics* 1253a2–3.

p.33 "Man is more given ..."
Nicomachean Ethics 1162a17–18.

p.35 "All men naturally ..."
Metaphysics 980a22.

p.38 "A man whom it is ..." A line from Aristotle's epitaph on Plato, cited by Olympiodorus, *Commentary on Plato's Gorgias* 41.9.

p.39 "Plato is dear to me ..." In this precise form, the aphorism is found in an ancient *Life of Aristotle*, but it is based on *Nicomachean Ethics* 1096a16–17 (where Aristotle is imitating Plato's remarks on Homer at *Republic* 595C).

p.40 he called me "... the belly." The story is found in Aelian, *Historical Miscellany* iv 9.

p.66 "Nature does nothing in vain" *On the Heavens* 291b13–14.

p.139 Postscript Text in *Sylloge Inscriptionum Graecarum* no.275, or in O. Gigon (ed.), *Aristotelis Opera*, III (Berlin, 1987), p.547.

REFILL?

Aristotle's major works—*Analytics*, *Ethics*, *Metaphysics*, *Physics*, *On the Soul*—have each been translated many times into English. They are available in a variety of paperback editions. All Aristotle's surviving works, in English translation, are collected in *The Complete Works of Aristotle*, edited by Jonathan Barnes (Princeton NJ: Princeton University Press, 1984).

There are several general discussions of Aristotle's thought, among them:

J.L. Ackrill, *Aristotle the Philosopher* (Oxford and New York: Oxford University Press, 1981)

D.J. Allan, *The Philosophy of Aristotle* (Oxford and New York: Oxford University Press, 1952)

J. Barnes, *Aristotle—A Very Short Introduction* (Oxford and New York: Oxford University Press, 2000)

J. Lear, *Aristotle: The Desire to Understand* (Cambridge and New York: Cambridge University Press, 1988)

W.D. Ross, *Aristotle* (London: Methuen, 1923)

Since antiquity, scholars and philosophers have commented upon and criticized Aristotle's ideas. In *The Cambridge Companion to Aristotle*, edited by Jonathan Barnes (Cambridge and New York: Cambridge University Press, 1995), there are chapters on most aspects of Aristotle's philosophy, and there is an extensive bibliography which may serve as a guide to more advanced reading.

INDEX